What Color Is
Your Parody?

Other Books by Charlie Haas

What Color Is Your Parrot Suit?
A Guide for Masqueraders and Trick-or-Treaters

What Color Is Your Paris Boot?
A Guide to French Shoe Fashions

What Color Is Your Parasite?
A Guide to Trichinosis and Tapeworm

What Color Is Your Paraffin?
A Guide for Jelly Canners and Candle Dippers

What Color Is Your Paramour?
A Guide to Interracial Dating

What Color Is Your Paraclete?
A Guide for Visionary Mystics

What Color Is Your Paramecium?
A Guide for Cell-Splitters and Slide-Gazers

What Color Is Your Parakeet?
A Guide for Cage-Cleaners and Feeder-Fillers

What Color Is Your Parody?

A Self-Harm Manual for Job-Hunters & Career-Changers

Charlie Haas

PRICE/STERN/SLOAN
Publishers, Inc., Los Angeles
1984

SECOND PRINTING — JUNE 1984

Copyright© 1984 by Charlie Haas
Published by Price/Stern/Sloan Publishers, Inc.
410 North La Cienega Boulevard, Los Angeles, California 90048

ISBN: 0-8431-0796-0

WHY THIS BOOK WAS WRITTEN,
COMMONLY CALLED

THE COME-ON,
OR STING

As I write these words, it is both a good time and a bad time in the world of job-hunting and career-changing. It is a good time in the sense that it is late Wednesday afternoon, following several Black Russians—a propitious moment to begin composing an unbelievably sincere book about how to find a job, and to fill up the

**Brands of cheap liquor favored by members
of overpopulated professional fields.**

blank spaces in that book with cute engravings scissored out of old collections whose copyrights have long since expired.

But it is a bad time to be looking for a new job or a new career. Cold, precise statistics tell the grim story: lots and lots of people are out of work, and a number of them have even given up looking.

For new college graduates, the job market is especially trouble-some and unpromising. In the last five years, according to surveys, fully 40 percent of persons earning legal and medical degrees or MBAs have become Skid Row alcoholics *within six months* of receiving these degrees, due to the lack of available positions. (See graph.)

This is a terrible human tragedy. Surely no humane, decent person can take pleasure in the prospect of tens of thousands of newly trained and accredited lawyers being without work, when it's so clear that more lawyers are what our society so desperately needs. The specter of countless sharp-tongued young balls of fire sitting in laundromats and circling want ads for fry cooks when they could be tying up people's lives with months of litigation would gladden the heart of only the most perverse and antisocial observer (and then only after several Black Russians).

The national unemployment picture, then, is a deeply upsetting thing. Does this book promise some sort of "magic formula," some quick-fix, sure-fire, wave-a-wand solution that will guaran-tee you a job? As a matter of fact, it does, but only if you have purchased one of the Lucky Books, in which the magic formula appears in place of one of the winsome illustrations. If this is not a Lucky Book, just keep buying copies and reading them till you find the right one. No problem.

But even without a Lucky Book or a magic formula, the employment picture is not nearly as bleak as it may seem. Millions of job vacancies are going unfilled, partly because so many job applicants have been bludgeoned by street criminals and left bleeding in alleys, a frequent occurrence in neighborhoods where job interviews are held. *Don't let this put you off.* Not only are there jobs to be had but, in "sunrise industries" such as computer technology and self-help book scamming, jobs and business opportunities are being *created* by people with drive and vision, and Alger Hiss-type success stories abound. Take Steve War-sawpact, an inventor-entrepreneur in California's Silicon Valley.

"I had heard this place was a real high-technology Mecca," says Steve, "and sure enough, when I got here, guys were flying around on carpets, talking Arabic, and praying five, maybe six times a day. I was real impressed!"

But not too impressed to go to work. When job openings in the area turned out to be few, Steve started his own company. New companies in Silicon Valley are traditionally started in garages, but Steve, who was living in an efficiency apartment, started his in his toaster oven. "The hottest product out here, of course, is the personal computer," he says. But by talking to a number of people who had bought them, Steve discovered that many manufacturers had gone overboard and made their computers *too* personal. "The machines were starting to make little remarks about the users' weight, or their choice of friends, even their sex lives. It gives you the creeps, you know, you try and read up a spreadsheet for a six-month profit projection, and the thing starts in, 'Mm, been into the Häagen-Dazs, have we?' "

Working tirelessly for six months of eighteen-hour days, and having to stop often when melting cheese impaired circuitry functions, Warsawpact finally perfected his Impersonal Computer, which runs his own VisiCouth software, boasts a "user-distant" keyboard, and has a 248-Kilobyte file in which to store things better left unsaid. An instant success, especially with balding and/or large-breasted middle managers, the IC has enabled Steve Warsawpact to buy a condo at Lake Tahoe and, for that matter, a taco at Lake Como.

Thus we see that, even in these difficult times, people are still finding new jobs and devising new careers for themselves. In almost every case, the people who are doing this are the *enthusiastic* job-hunters, who have applied the techniques in this book: techniques not only useful during good times, but during Depressions as well. In fact, these skills are *especially* useful during Depressions, which is why there are long sections on job opportunities in vaudeville, Fiestaware design, and Atwater-Kent radio repair.

In their simplest form, the important points to remember about job-hunting are these:

(1) *You improve your chances of finding a job once you take the limiting, pigeonholing labels off yourself.* Do not say, "I am a convicted forger, I am semiliterate, I pour a cup of Jack Daniel's on my Product 19 to start the day." Instead say, "I am gifted in graphics, I am not hung up on verbal concepts, I have interesting recipe ideas."

(2) *You improve your chances of finding a job when you are observant and resourceful.* Perhaps you, like other decent, caring, talented people, have seen the little notices in magazines that read, "Please patronize our advertisers." Perhaps you have skipped past these notices, never realizing that they constitute one of the

most desirable job offers in existence! Many magazines are looking for people to pose as customers at prestige stores and restaurants and behave in a patronizing manner toward the proprietors, so that these business people will not get overconfident and ignore the need for continued advertising. Imagine walking into stores such as Saks Fifth Avenue and muttering to the managers, "I don't suppose you'd actually have anything decent enough to wear around this quaint little dump," waltzing out with a smirk on your face—*and getting paid for it!* The good jobs are out there—but you have to be on your toes.

(3) *A job is like car keys, or a scarf: You find it in the last place you look.* Does this mean that your job might be under the bed? Surprisingly, it could mean just that, since many people report that serving as a gigolo to wealthy golf widows is an excellent job, usually performed indoors and with very little heavy lifting, that frequently does find them under the bed, staring at Perfect Sleeper mattress fire warning tags—and holding very still.

(4) *You improve your chances of finding a job when you know what you have to offer a potential employer.* Some employers respond to rocks of cocaine the size of softballs, while others respond to semi-automatic small arms fire.

(5) *You improve your chances of finding a job when you use techniques such as "networking."* True, setting up a nationwide hookup of television stations may seem like an elaborate solution to your problem. On the other hand, even *with* the continual abysmal showing of NBC-TV in the ratings, you haven't bumped into Brandon Tartikoff down at the food stamp distribution center lately, have you?

(6) *You improve your chances of getting a job if you cultivate an air of extreme menace.* The curled lip, the time-bomb eyes, the primal hunched shoulders. Many job-hunters like to study Clint Eastwood's performances in the *Dirty Harry* pictures in order to develop this vital faculty.

(7) *You improve your chances of finding a job when you are a major stockholder during a hostile takeover situation.* "Yes, yes, that tender offer of five million dollars sounds fine, but what I'd really like is a good shot at an entry-level position with on-the-job training and dental benefits." What kind of acquisition-hungry CEO would say no to that sort of straight talk?

(8) *Successful careers go to people who see the full potential in an industry or enterprise.* Four years ago, my friend Tony was a bartender at a dive in suburban Minneapolis. But he had taken note of the success of franchised chain businesses that used celebrity names as "drawing cards." Today, Tony runs a growing chain of cocktail lounges called Peter Fonda's Blackout. He realized what a little initiative, and a little marketing, could do.

(9) *You increase your chances of finding a job if you are white and male.* Affirmative action programs are part of the picture these days, it's true, but this "old standby" of job-hunting isn't going anywhere. Work at being white and male. Don't worry about the "how" of it. The important thing, as with all aspects of job-hunting, is to be *persistent* and *dedicated*.

(10) *You improve your chances of finding a job if you treat job-hunting itself as a job, to be worked at.* The search for a job is a 40-hour-a-week affair, and you are your own boss. So get to it: Humiliate yourself in front of other people. Submit expense accounts to yourself and question half the items on them. Complain to your spouse about yourself. Lie awake half the night

composing indignant letters to yourself in your head. Go to dinner at your own house, get drunk, make a pass at your spouse, apologize, become maudlin, and then act especially distant toward yourself for several days thereafter. Get to it *now*.

(11) *You improve your chances of finding a job when you know what makes you different from other people in your line of work.* Is your notion of ethics particularly fanciful? Are you quick to notice, and report, the shortcomings of other employees? Are

you willing to let an immediate superior take credit for at least 65 percent of your ideas? If your job is at a desk, can you make paper-clip chains with one hand, leaving the other free to doodle cubes, dollar signs and naked torsos? Is your figure less than Greek? Is your mouth a little weak? When you open it to speak, are you smart? By letting a potential employer know what's special about you, you give yourself a head start against other applicants for the same position, increasing the likelihood that their hopes will be crushed, their self-esteem diminished, their family weakened— rather than yours.

The job-hunting techniques in this book are *not* just for white-collar job hunters, nor for blue-collar—they've been proven to work for everybody. Young job-hunters. Old job-hunters. Urban job-hunters. Rural job-hunters. Job-hunters with freckles. Job-hunters without freckles. Job-hunters who pack it to the right when they dress, and job-hunters who pack it to the left. Job-hunters who remember Mario Lanza. Job-hunters with kind of webbing between their toes so it almost looks like the little webbed feet on a duck or something. Job-hunters who hum a little tune when they're swabbing their ears so they can hear it reverberate around in there, and job-hunters who don't. All kinds of job-hunters.

If there's one thing I've learned in the time we've been publishing and updating this excellent book, it's this: anyone, anywhere, who gets a job does it by using the same resources that are found in this book—old engravings; droll comic strips and cartoons; and smarmy New Age homilies. "Double-entry bookkeeping and CRT operation are perfectly good skills," I've heard countless employers say, "but an applicant who knows an Albrecht Dürer from a Currier & Ives, or can quote the punchlines of old Garfield strips, or who goes around talking like an old issue of the *Whole Earth Catalogue*—that's the kind of person I'm going to hire nine times out of ten."

Finding a job is one of the hardest, most repetitive, most dispiriting things you'll ever have to do. But there are ways of going about it, and that's what this book is all about. In addition, there are ways of feeling better *now*, while you're looking. For example, just think how you'll feel once you find that job. If your job is like 80 percent of the jobs in America, surveys show, you're likely to find the work pointless, demeaning, or both; and you're even more likely to consider yourself underpaid, mistreated, and regarded as a human doormat by people with about one-fifth your intelligence. Your companions on the job may very well include people who stick cute little "You Don't Have to Be Crazy to Work Here, But It Helps" signs on their acoustic partitions, and people who tell you the entire plots of made-for-TV movies in precise detail over lunch at Burger Chef. It will be a torturous daily struggle to bring yourself to go to work. When that time comes, you'll very likely look back on this job-hunting period, when you wanted a job so badly, and say, "Ha! That's a good one on me! I must have been out of my mind!"

Feel better already, don't you?

Go get 'em, tiger,

Charlie Haas
January, 1984

P.S.–Given the presence of millions of women in today's job market and recent social changes with regard to sex roles, only a brutal buffoon would persist in sexist language usage, an outmoded habit that devalues men and women alike. Therefore, all references to "hot personnel department bimbos with hooters that just won't quit" and "brawny hunk office managers whose strapping thighs in their tight Sansabelts promise unimagined ecstasy" have been considerably toned down for this edition.

*"Give a man a fish,
and he can eat for a day.
But teach a man how to fish,
and he'll be dead of mercury
poisoning inside of three
years."*

—Fitzhugh Tuoti

CHAPTER ONE

Job-Hunting: More Fun Than the Bunny Hop!

Well, here you are.
  Lying on the couch, half-blind
  With icy, nauseous terror
 At the prospect of getting up, going into
 The other room, putting on your support hose and dickey
And so forth, and going out
To look for a job. Every time you think
About the rejection and humiliation
You're going to experience, looking for a job
Out there, you feel another wave of anguish
 Roll through your vital organs in an involuntary spasm,
 And you wish for death,
  But death doesn't come,
    and here you are. It's a good thing
    You have this book to buck you up
      And encourage you,
        Or things might begin to look grim.
        So you pull yourself together
          (Make sure you get the feet on the right legs)—
            Ha! That's just an example
             Of the folksy, homespun kind of humor
              This book uses
                To make you feel so much better.
                  A lot of my friends say
                   I should be a stand-up comedian,
                     But then who would update the Job-Hunting
                     Resource Directory
                     At the back of this book every year,
                     Taking out all the counseling services
                     That have been busted?
                     Anyway, this isn't supposed to be about *my* problems,
                    This is *your* chapter, designed to help you think
                  About *your* problems. Maybe *you* should be
                A stand-up comedian. But first, you have
                To stand up.

          So you start going about the business
          Of looking for a job. Maybe not even
         Any special *kind* of job, like wax or snow
        Or grease or blow, but just a job. You take a look
       At the want ads, first of all

Because that is where people look
   When they want a job,
      So let's take a look together, let's open up the—
         Hey! When did they start putting the "Jumble" puzzle
            In the want ads? I haven't done this sucker
               In ages. I thought they'd dropped it
                  Completely. "NOYIMH," what the hell is
                  "NOYIMH?" Boy, some days you can do the whole thing
                     In your head in about twelve seconds,
                     And some days you stare
                      And stare and stare and stare
                      At one of these words
                      For twenty minutes, does you no good
                      At all. Oh, "hominy," okay. Actually,
                      It's harder than it looks, making up the "Jumble,"
                        Because the anagrams can't be anagrams of two different words,
                     Did you ever think of that?
                  I kind of admire those guys
               That do it.
            I'm pretty good at the crossword puzzles too,
         Except not those weird
      English ones, I mean,
   "Tay-Sachs victim does the bolero pretty darn
Quick, you bet!" What the fuck kind of definition
Is that? But the *New York Times* one is good for
Killing half the morning. You'll be glad to know that
If you ever do get a job. Hey, that's right,
This is *your* chapter, *your* book, about getting
You a job and trying to salvage the
Nine-county federal disaster area you've made out of
Your life. (Just a little more homespun humor there.)

   Well, it's *hard*, looking for a job.
      That's why you have to keep at it, and not
         Let anything distract you.
            Still, sometimes it's so hard
               That when some low-normal Nazi cretin
                  Of a personnel director has told you

That you can't have the job
  Because you're "over-qualified,"
    Or because you're "a poor security risk
    After that business with the Bulgarians
      And the microfilm," or because you're "dumb
      As a post," sometimes it just makes you
        Want to sneak back into his office at night
        With a jar of fish essence
        (From a gourmet food store)
        And leave an invisible coat of it
        Under some randomly chosen object
        So the smell will drive him out of his
        Third-rate mind,
        And he won't be able to get rid of it
        Without burning everything.
      I know. I've been there too. (Get
    The three-ounce size. The Scotch Tape dispenser
  Is a good target.) But the thing about looking
    For a job is,
  You have to keep at it, in fact you have to get to it
Right *now*. But the want ads aren't any good,
  They all seem to be about
  Free abortion counseling or
Discount trips to Mr. Sy's Casino of Fun
In Las Vegas. So you put the want ads aside
And you start talking to some friends of yours
Who have jobs, to see if—
What? Oh, come on,
You must have *one* friend with a job.
  Boy, the kind of people who go out and buy this book,
    I'm telling you, you should see my mail,
      There are some prize Yo-Yo's walking around
        Out there, real Duncan Imperials, with handwriting
        Like a psycho killer. Really, I'm serious.
        Ha! Just kidding again!

        So you go see your friend Ralph,
          Who has a job
            As an Assistant Administrative Group Head
            At a Fortune 500 corporation,

And you say, "Ralph, I've always wanted to be
An Assistant Administrative Group Head, I mean,
Even when I was a little kid,
And people asked me what I wanted
To be when I grew up,
I would say, 'Wanna be a 'sistant mini-strative
Group head, 'cause they get to *prioritize*.'
"Do you think," you ask, a little nervously,
"That I *could* be one?" And Ralph says,
"Well, I think there are a number of parameters
That we want to look at here,
And bring into play,
In terms of the overall,
So we can begin to work out a sort of
Frame of reference,
Because we're dealing with some modes of data **upstreaming**
And integrating several strata
Of service sectors, so you have an upside
Market penetration dynamic as well as
Full vertical liaising capability."

"Whew!" you say, "this job-hunting is thirsty work!"
And you swing over to the La Barca Lounge,
By the Interstate there, for a couple quick
Ones. Not a bad idea, actually. There's
Such a thing as taking this job-hunting stuff
Too seriously. I know of some people
Who have actually developed severe mental problems
Due to the extreme pressure and frustration
Which studies have shown to be associated
With the job-hunting process. One day
They're living a totally normal life, going
To job interviews, kiting checks,
Jamming the gas meter,
And the next day they're down at the happy place,
Chatting up the wallpaper and staring into
Their chocolate milk. We don't want that
Happening to you, so when you're out there
Job-hunting, make sure you don't
Suddenly develop any aberrational thought patterns,
Delusions, or hysterical tendencies.
Or even any "strange feelings."
Actually, there's probably nothing to worry about
Yet. If you were really starting to "lose it,"
As clinical psychologists say,
There'd be some pretty definite
Problems with your grip on reality, like
You'd be looking at this poem I'm writing,
Where all the lines are neatly and evenly
Lined up down the left-hand side of the page,
And you'd start to think that they were slinking
Down the page in some kind of curve,
Like a snake, which would be only the first sign
Of a condition where you'd be seeing snakes
Everywhere, coming to bite you. Like
You might start worrying that there was one
In your glove compartment,
Right now. And then you'd think,
"Oh, that's silly, how would a snake
Get in my glove compartment?"

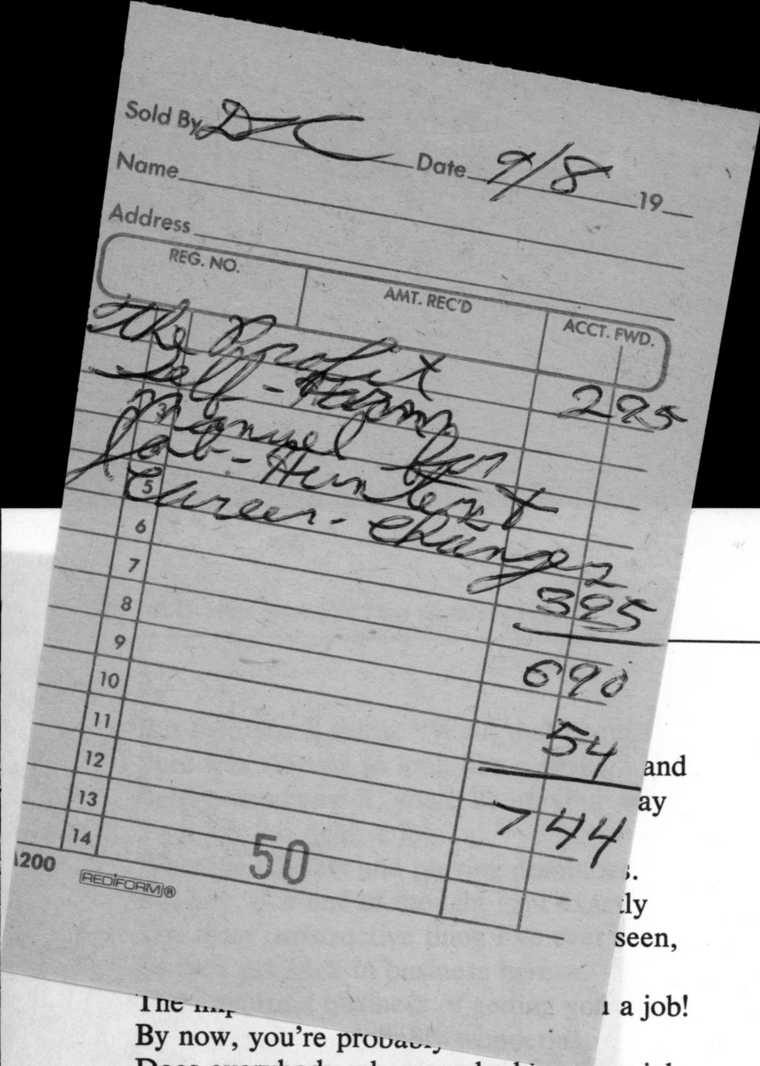

and
ay
s.
ly
seen,
The ... a job!
By now, you're prob...
Does everybody who goes looking for a job
Get thiss disscouraged and frussstrated,
Sssso that thingsss really ssstart to look
Hopelesss? Well, my friend,
I'm afraid the anssswer issss,
HISSSSS!

HISSSSS!

HISSSSS!

*"Be nice to the people you
meet on the way to the top,
because they'll probably be
called as witnesses when you're
indicted for price-fixing,
union busting and insider
stock dumping."*

—Anonymous

CHAPTER TWO

You're Already Blowing It!

A well-known writer on careers and employment has said that the job-finding process can be summarized as NO NO NO NO NO NO NO NO NO YES. This may be true in some cases, although an increasingly accurate rendering in present times would be NO NO NO NO NO NO NO NO NO NO NO NO NO NO NO NO NO NO NO WHY IS THAT GUY OUT THERE ON THE LEDGE WHAT IS HE DOING OH MY GOD HE SAID HE WAS GOING TO I DIDN'T BELIEVE HIM OH MY GOD OH MY GOD DOES OUR INSURANCE COVER US?

Why should this be so? It is so because of the nature of the job placement system in our country—a system that is not only outdated and soul-destroying but dishonest and probably illegal, a system worse than feudalism, worse than Ticketron, worse than if the MIRV missile launchers were wired to the answer buzzers on *Hollywood Squares*. Most of the practices by which people acquire jobs in this country are ruthless, underhanded shams. If you are like most readers of this book, you will fit right in.

Perhaps the inequities and inefficiencies of our employment system wouldn't be so crucially harmful if our society didn't place such an exaggerated value on occupation and achievement, as if a person's salary and title were somehow of more importance than his good dental hygiene habits or his uncanny impression of James Mason in *North by Northwest*.

Fortunately, there have recently been some signs of improvement in our society's attitude toward work and "selfhood." As employment consultant Bea Nephew wrote in a recent article, "Not so many years ago, in a less enlightened time, the lack of a prestigious job made you somehow 'less of a man.' Today, if you don't have a prestigious job, you may be somehow 'less of a man' *or* somehow 'less of a woman.' That's progress."

But by any measure, our way of putting people together with jobs is woefully outmoded. Studies show that over 35 percent of male personnel directors have haircuts of the sort associated with Dana Andrews and favor Old Spice cologne, while close to half of all female personnel directors have their eyeglasses on those little chains of fake pearls. Most damning of all, the median magazine in employment agency waiting areas is a 1971 issue of *U.S. News and World Report* with a cover story claiming that granola had caused laboratory rats to grow wispy little beards and quote Kurt Vonnegut.

"It's a numbers game," admitted one unusually frank employment counselor, who asked not be be identified—"this could get me fired in a minute if they ever found out who it was." This counselor, who works in the largest city of the "Show Me" state, drives a tan 1982 Chevrolet Caprice and has two children aged eight and twelve, said from under his red moustache, "The agencies view each applicant as just another number. With luck, you might get to be a prime, a power of ten, or at least something in a nice Fibonacci series. But I've seen too many people—talented people, enthusiastic people—come in here and find themselves perceived as just another bland integer you'd count right past without a second thought. It does something to people's spirits. It's dehumanizing."

And what happens to these people who are turned into numbers by employment agencies? Inevitably, they fill out forms, write resumes, go for interviews, and—in the worst cases—find jobs. Why "the worst cases"? Because the most dismaying aspect of our employment system is not its clumsiness, its duplication of effort, or even its role in bringing forth books like this one. The worst aspect of our system is that people find jobs through it—dumb jobs, dull jobs, jobs where a grotesque, anal-retentive fetish is made of things like "showing up on time" and "staying around for a full shift," where neo-fascistic "lines of command" are set up by "executives" and "managers," jobs where phrases like "trouble-shooting" and "long-range planning" are used by people with perfectly straight faces—in short, jobs where the whole business of "work" is blown up out of all reasonable proportion. In a blue-collar version of such a job, you might spend your whole day jamming car parts together with nothing to do for amusement but weld half a sandwich into the door of some sucker's Camaro or LTD; in the white-collar version, you might spend as much as an hour and forty-five minutes imprisoned in a "meeting" without hearing a single dialect joke and with nothing more bracing to drink than acid-neutralized Kava. Either way, not a pretty picture.

If you are content to hunt for a dumb job, this is not the book for you. Why don't we just get that out in the open right now and agree to an amicable parting of the ways, saving ourselves a lot of grief and ugly public displays down the line? I want the Miles Davis records, though. I *bought* those records. Some people. Unbelievable. Jesus Christ.

The trick, then, is to find yourself a smart job. And, yes, there are some out there. They may not be in the classified ads or in the employment agency listings; you may have to look hard, using some imagination, in order to find them, because they are special and desirable. But they are worth the effort, and *you can do it*, if you *get to it now*. Here are just a few of the smart jobs in today's market:

PRIZE STROKER

As a job seeker, you probably have a good working familiarity with daytime television game shows. If not, *commit* several hours a day to acquiring that familiarity, starting *now*. Not only do these programs, through their questions, educate you in general knowledge and, through their prizes, keep you informed about the world of commerce and popular taste—all of which can be crucial in your job-hunt—but they also feature practitioners of an exciting, opportunity-packed profession. As unseen announcers introduce rewards such as Samsonite luggage, Amana Touchmatic Radar-Ranges and Mercury Lynxes, the prize strokers—cheerful, attractive young women of the sort you'd be proud to have over for sour cream-onion soup dip and Bailey's Irish Cream—run their hands all over these prizes so that viewers will be assured that these prizes are real, and not cheap holographic projections. This is the very essence of a smart job: though there is nothing involved that could be even remotely described as work, the money is excellent, the hours brief, and the activity itself so weirdly amusing that it enables the job-holder to save on drugs.

"It's even more sensational than I thought it would be," says Ginchy Bauble, a prize stroker on a major midmorning show. "I mean, for a job, it really has a lot of sensational features that should be pointed out one at a time so that nobody misses them." But how does one set about to enter this fast-track field? "Oh, well, I guess it was always my ambition, even as a little girl. Betty Furness, I would say, was the closest thing to a hero that I had, you know, a role model, when I was growing up—apart from my mother, of course. My mom had this terrific way of dusting things, which I think has really influenced my style. Well, of course, at that time, there was no place to study prize stroking *per se*—I understand you can now minor in it at certain colleges around L.A., which I think is a terrific thing for the young people coming up, but then, well, you were really on your own. But I came out here to live, and I met Miss Furness, who was very encouraging, and of course Bernadette Castro, who's been kind of a mentor to me and a lot of other people, helping us along. There's a lot that goes into it that people don't realize, like, okay, pointing out the sensational features on a prize, the way you keep your wrist pointed and you use just the first two fingers—you may not be aware of these things, but if they weren't done correctly, it could take away from your enjoyment, believe me."

GUN-RUNNER IN MACAO

Where you could wind up missing as easily as you wind your watch, where you're always just one step ahead of the footsteps behind you, where "trust" is a joke that stopped being funny about a hundred dockside fistfights ago, where the thieves and whores and opium junkies are the "country club set." Sure there's danger, sure you could be applying for a job as piranha food every time you go down another dark backstreet to make another dark deal with the side that pays the most. But it beats hell out of punching a time clock back where the biggest adventure is a rush-hour commute across the G.W. Bridge, am I right or am I right? Yeah, you bet your ass I'm right. You weren't planning on living forever, or were you? Nah. You light up a Park Lane, squinting against the smoke with the dead eyes of one who has seen too much, and you wait for the junk with its running lights off to bring in another little consignment of heap-strong-firesticks for the rebels who'd sell you out in a second if you weren't their only hope of taking the capital before they run out of money for ammo. A nice slot as a junior exec at Doyle Dane? Thanks but no thanks.

RECLUSIVE ECCENTRIC BILLIONAIRE

Yes, it's a plum position, but don't go ruling it out. Remember that major American corporations in several diverse fields—aviation, casino management, motion picture production, land development and undersea exploration—have turned to this kind of individual both for managerial acumen and for priceless publicity value. "But I don't have the fear of germs," you say. Banana oil, I say—are you telling me you *like* germs? You had some germs *over* last week? You just ordered some diphtheria toxin by mail? "Well, no . . ." Then what's the hangup? "Oh, I just don't know if I can grow my fingernails that long." Drink some gelatin and *quit whining*. This is one of the smartest jobs going, but you have to go after it *now*.

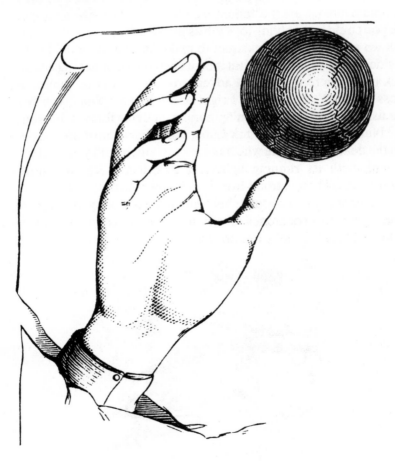

DEWAR'S PROFILE SCOUT

Everyone's seen those magazine advertisements for Dewar's White Label scotch, in which go-getters in various fields are "Profiled," with attention to their accomplishments, choice of reading matter, personal credo, and, of course, favorite whiskey. But have you ever stopped to think about how the Dewar's people find these paragons? Klaus "The Human Barfly" Bierback did, and now he has one of the smartest jobs possible: a Dewar's Profile Talent Scout. "There's a lot of travel," says Klaus. "Basically the drill is to go to a major city, check into the best hotel and start hitting the classiest bars in town. When I see someone really photogenic order Dewar's, I go over and start buying them drinks and chatting them up. If they're a claims adjuster, or if I can see that their best quote is going to be something like, 'What the hell, they'll probably drop the fucking bomb on all of us tomorrow,' I just thank them for their time and move on. Those aphorism-coining microsurgeons are out there, and not all of them drink Johnnie Walker Black by any means, but it takes a certain amount of patience, and a *lot* of drinking. But is this a great job, or what? I'd recommend it to anyone." Klaus notes that he's never yet had an unsuccessful trip, except to Mexico City, where heavy drinking at high altitudes caused him to succumb to incapacitating fits of laughter—a condition known to tourists as "Cantinflas's Revenge."

DANGER SIGNS OF DUMB JOBS

Routing slips
Desk caddies
Hold buttons
Wednesday morning
   creative group
   meetings
Paging beepers
Team spirit
Pendaflex files
Post-Its
Follow-up memos
Sales presentations
Working lunches
Prayer breakfasts
Coffee stations with
   non-dairy creamer and
   single-serving dehydrated
   soups
Chargebacks
Working capital
Suggestion boxes
Cost control
"From the desk of" pads
Stress management
Dale Carnegie courses
30-day billing
"This pen stolen from" pens
Strategy conferences at
   Airport Hiltons

Product line extension
Market share
Volume buying
Desk blotters
Paper cuts
Motivational training
   filmstrips
Promotional tie-ins
Purchase order numbers
Daytimer calendars
FICA
LIFO
FIFO
Overhead projectors
Drop-shipping
Off-loading
Jet-Paks
Payroll Savings Plan
Cross-collateralization
Quality circles
Discount Family Fun
   Day at Marriott's
   Great America
Rolodex
Filofax
Telex
NYNEX
Wordstar
Work

*"If anything can go
wrong involving cabbage
and mayonnaise, it will."*

(Cole's Law)

CHAPTER THREE

What Do You Want to Do, and to Whom?

So now you know that there are jobs worth going after and jobs not even worth a second thought. "Where," you ask, "do I go from here? How do I begin my progress into the exhilarating world of job applications and face-to-face interviews, so that I too may have a smart job one day?"

"Not so fast," is, if course, the answer. If there's one thing I've learned in my long weeks of professional experience in this field, it's this:

> You have to decide what your skills are, and what you want to use them for, or you will wind up writing self-help books.

In this chapter, we're going to do some simple exercises to determine what your skills are and, at the same time, "turn you on," as today's young people say, to some resources that can help you turn these skills into a job.

To many people, the word "skills" is a bugaboo. To others, it's a shibboleth; to still others, it's a sort of palimpsest. But in fact, there's nothing mysterious about skills, and almost everybody has a few. The important thing to remember is that, as the chart on this page demonstrates, all skills involve interaction with *data, things, or people*.

THE THREE TYPES OF SKILLS

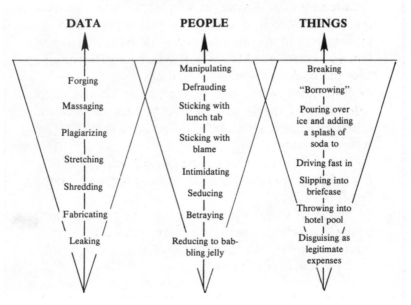

DATA	PEOPLE	THINGS
Forging	Manipulating	Breaking
Massaging	Defrauding	"Borrowing"
Plagiarizing	Sticking with lunch tab	Pouring over ice and adding a splash of soda to
Stretching	Sticking with blame	Driving fast in
Shredding	Intimidating	Slipping into briefcase
Fabricating	Seducing	Throwing into hotel pool
Leaking	Betraying	Disguising as legitimate expenses
	Reducing to babbling jelly	

After you've studied the Skills Chart and done Practical Exercise Number One, you'll be ready to fill in the "PICTURE OF THE JOB I AM LOOKING FOR" chart on page 41. Often, just showing this chart to a personnel director is enough to cinch your deal. But should actual resumes and interviews be necessary, the information in the next three chapters will turn these trying experiences into one long song—a song co-authored by Barry Manilow, Billy Joel, Jacques Brel and Anthony Newley.

PRACTICAL EXERCISE #1:
MEET YOUR JOB SKILLS

1. Go to a library that has a good selection of reference books on jobs and occupations. Take a notebook along.

2. With the notebook on a table, sit in a chair with knees pointed outward at 45 degrees and feet flat on floor. Keeping back straight, try to reach the far edge of the table. Repeat ten times. (This part of the exercise is good for shoulders, chest, forearms.)

3. In the notebook, write down a description of every positive work experience you have had so far, with a detailed account of your responsibilities and what you feel you learned from the job, as well as people on the job who impressed you as strong workers, and what you feel you contributed to each place where you worked. Use the back of the page if necessary.

4. Still sitting, with hands on hips, stretch from side to side, keeping back straight. Try to touch head to tabletop. Repeat 15 times. (This part of exercise tones hips and tummy.)

5. Make a list of everyone you can still borrow money from. If list is shorter than 10 names, proceed to number 6.

6. Stand up. Reach *back behind you* with your hands, trying to touch the floor. Fall over into bookshelf. Hurt back. Sue library. Collect large settlement. Forget job-hunting nonsense. Throw big party.

RESOURCE #1:

GOVERNMENT PUBLICATIONS

The U.S. Government Printing Office publishes a number of career-guidance pamphlets that many job-hunters find helpful. A complete list can be obtained by writing to the GPO in Washington, but the following sample is representative of popular titles:

Easy Duns It: Careers in Bill Collection
Your Mama Liked It: Making Money With Antiques
Don't Get Sore, Get Sorghum!
It's "In Form" to Inform: Helping Government
    Agencies Keep Track of Your Friends
Mail-Order Molybdenum Means Mucho Mazuma!
And That's Vinyl: The Plastic Slipcover Bonanza!

Creosote and You: A Natural Match
What Hath God Wrought-Iron: Decorative Window
    Bars Spell P-R-O-F-I-T-S
Jojoba's Witnesses: True Stories of the Miracle Bean!
Update: Under the Reagan administration, the GPO has discontinued the above titles, replacing them with a single pamphlet for job-hunters, entitled *Fuck Off and Die.*

RESOURCE #2:

PEOPLE WHO CAN HELP YOU GET ESTABLISHED AS A GUN-RUNNER IN MACAO

His Scariness Col. Moammar Khadafy
Qaddifi House
Avenue de Kadaffi
Tripoli, Libya

The Last Two Guys from the Weather
    Underground
A Leftish Lawyer's Guest Room
Connecticut

The Friendly Union of Patriotic American Nice
    Iranian Students Studying a Lot, You Bet
Royce Hall
University of California at Los Angeles

The My Sinn Fein Ladies' Fragrance and
    Fund-Raising Circle
South Boston, Massachusetts

Suzie's Uzis and Fuses for Druzes
Ask around, but be, you know,
halfway fucking cool about it
Tangier, Morocco

Wilson and Terpil, Consultants
Industrial Park of No Return
Langley, Virginia

RESOURCE #3:

VULNERABLE AREAS OF KEY PERSONNEL DIRECTORS

Mr. Franklin Dunsmuir
Wippee Products Corp.
Carageenan, Ohio
Ask if *all* executives at Wippee have a year's supply of
ladies' black hose in their right-middle desk drawers.

Ms. Estelle Toth
E-Z-Lux Winch Co.
Pause, Utah
Slip ten bucks to the desk clerk at the Discreet Retreet
Motel out on Hildebrand some Wednesday at 2:00
for an interesting "photo opportunity."

Mr. Lance Potemkin
Mir-a-Kill Roach Powder
Edema, Texas
"I understand you were a Navy man, Mr. Potemkin . . .
say, what *did* become of the rest of that unit you were
in?"

Mr. Milt Hanky
Lustre-Sheen Lunch Meats, Inc.
Lazenby, North Carolina
Catch him in *Major Barbara* at the dinner theater over
the Lazenby Lanes and tell him he was fantastic. It
won't kill you.

Ms. Cora Postum
Can-Do Fondue Fork Works
Meteskey, New Jersey.
"I hear you're really *whipping* things into shape around
here, Miz Postum . . . I mean really *spurring* the
people on, so you can *hog-tie* the competition . . . yes, I
hear it's a real hell-for-*leather* outfit you've got
here . . . ."

PRACTICAL EXERCISE #2:
THE QUICK SKILL-FINDING CHART

	I can do, because I have done:	Check if appropriate	Which suggests a job in:
1. Machine or Manual Skills	Pushing; shoving; tweaking; twiddling; squeezing; kneading; tying in a knot; tying in a bow; throwing over my shoulder like a Continental soldier		
	Breaking; busting; rending asunder; smashing into a jillion pieces; dropping		
	Diluting with baby laxative; diluting with talcum powder; cutting into short grams and selling to kids at Motley Crue concert		
	Leaving on too long; turning up too high; allowing to short out; allowing to burn house down		
	Revving up way past the red line in all four gears and scaring the shit out of all the nice families out on the streets by the mall		
2. Artistic Skills	Little balloon men; shadow rabbits during slide shows; pipe-cleaner animals		
	Macrame plant hangers; decoupage candy boxes; letting different colored candles drip all over wine bottles		
	Painting "El Loco Boy 127" on side of subway car		
	Hooking up psychedelic colored-light machine from Radio Shack to stereo		
	Engraving accurate likenesses of past presidents, national monuments, one-eyed pyramids and difficult foreign phrases such as "ANNUIT COEPTIS"		
3. Performing Skills	Boring a few people at a time		
	Boring large groups of people		
	Charades; smutty charades; hollow charades		
	Joke about blind guy and his dog at Bloomingdale's		
4. Persuasive Skills	Mulcting; euchring; prevailing; prevaricating; wheedling; bullying; stampeding		
	Getting someone else to take my shift		
	Getting someone else to fill out this chart		
	Talking paint off walls; selling ice in wintertime; charming pants off mannequin		
	Faking college education; faking cholera; faking remembering name of one-night stand in aisle of Lumber City; faking tapping foot to music of Michel Legrand		

5. Institutional and Leadership Skills	Willingness to delegate authority		
	Willingness to delegate blame		
	Conceiving of new products; new product development; contributing to living standard of inspectors from FTC or Agriculture Department in order to insure availability of new product to public; denying charges that new product caused children in New Mexico to turn orange and float away; dumping new product in Third World countries		
And I applied these skills with:	Aplomb		
	Discretion		
	A certain flair		
	A funny hat		
	Elan		
	Panache		
	Joie de vivre		
	Mise-en-scene		
	Boudin noir		

A PICTURE OF THE JOB I AM LOOKING FOR

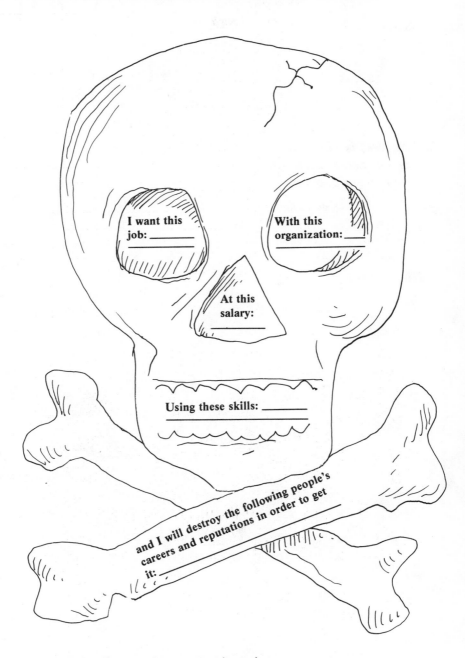

I want this job: _____

With this organization: _____

At this salary:

Using these skills: _____

and I will destroy the following people's careers and reputations in order to get it: _____

Fill out this chart, and present to interviewer when applying for a job.

"Success is ninety-nine percent perspiration and one percent poppers."

—Kalvin Kline

CHAPTER FOUR

The Resume: A "Rap Sheet" of Your Career

A resume, like a consomme, should be clear. Remember that the personnel executive who will read your resume is a busy, conscientious professional working hard at putting the right people into the right jobs. (It's not a bad idea, by the way, to familiarize yourself with the reference works commonly used by people who process resumes, particularly that big *Scientific American* book on the best designs for paper airplanes.)

On the following pages you'll find examples of the kind of resumes that get people jobs: concise, well-organized, readable. You would do well, when composing your own resume, to imitate these. You can even imitate the jobs on them, if you have to. Try and remember to use your own address, though.

UPTON FEHLER III
79 E. 65th Street
New York, N.Y. 10021
(212) 555-8341

JOB OBJECTIVE

Position in financial management or administration
position with a company on the way up, a "winning
team" with promising prospects for expansion, in-
creased market share, etc.

PROFESSIONAL EXPERIENCE

1980-1983	OSBORNE COMPUTER CORP. San Jose, Calif.
	Director of Product Position- ing, responsible for timing of new product introductions and identification of prod- ucts' positions in marketplace.
1979-1980	CAMBRIDGE DIET CO. Monterey, Calif. Vice President for Sales and Marketing, responsible for co- ordinating sales team efforts and developing incentive pro- grams.
1977-1979	BRANIFF AIRLINES Dallas, Tx. Senior Vice President for Route Planning, responsible for selecting and scheduling competitive flight routes
1975-1977	PENN SQUARE BANK Tulsa, Okla. Loan marketing executive, responsible for attracting new loan business to bank and coordinating with loan com- mittee.

Upton Fehler pg. 2

1973-1975   LOCKHEED AIRCRAFT CO.
                 Burbank, Calif.
                 Foreign Liaison Director, re-
                 sponsible for arrangement of
                 contracts with overseas clients.

1970-1973   PENN CENTRAL RAILROAD
                 Philadelphia, Pa.
                 Vice President for Passenger
                 Train Operations, manager of
                 large commuter train transpor-
                 tation system.

1962-1970   INVESTORS OVERSEAS SERVICES, LTD.
                 New York, N.Y.
                 Portfolio Supervisor, responsi-
                 ble for quality of investment
                 portfolio of mutual fund invest-
                 ment service

1958-1962   STUDEBAKER AUTOMOBILE CO.
                 South Bend, Ind.
                 Vice President for Projects
                 That Seemed Like a Good Idea
                 at the Time, with a wide range
                 of marketing and financial re-
                 sponsibilities

EDUCATION

1954-1958   Master of Business Administration
                 Van Doren College, Prestone, Pa.
                 (Now a Target Discount Store)

PERSONAL

Divorced. Excellent health. Interests include
World Football League memorabilia, 8-track tape
collection, mood jewelry.

This is an excellent example of the "business restrospective" format, in which career highlights occupy "center stage." A very comprehensive and impressive resume, likely to lead to employment.

```
                    Lena Overbrook
                    247 Camille Ln.
                 Times Beach, Mo. 63025
                    (314) 555-8701


POSITIONS SOUGHT: High-voltage wiring instal-
                  lation; aerial tramway main-
                  tenance; hazardous waste man-
                  agement; explosive disarming.

PREVIOUS EXPERIENCE


      1979-1984 DROPSY SLEEPING PILL CO.
                Baltimore, Md.
                Inventory Control Manager, re-
                sponsible for tracking quanti-
                ties of sleeping pills manufac-
                tured and packaged.

      1976-1979 SHIP-SHARP RAZOR BLADES, INC.
                St. Louis, Mo.
                Quality Control Director, re-
                sponsible for consistent sharp-
                ness of a line of single- and
                double-edged razor blades, dis-
                posable razors, etc.

      1971-1976 ROAST-MOST OVEN CO.
                Houston, Texas
                Inspection Supervisor, respon-
                sible for final inspections of
                large institutional gas ovens.


SALARY REQUIREMENTS

Negotiable.  My most important job objective
is to find a stable position in which I can
"settle down"; in short, I would like my next
job to be my last job, and money is not the
be-all and end-it-all, I mean end-all, of a
job as far as I am concerned.

PERSONAL

31 years old, unmarried.  Hobbies: Rock climbing,
hang-gliding, knot tying.  I will include further
details upon request, but at this point there
seems to be no reason to go on.
```

The resume on the previous page is a model one, especially in the writer's creditable willingness to take on difficult assignments. The employer who hires this applicant will have more than just an employee—he or she will have a friend for life.

ANTHONY "THE FERRET" AVENGIO
90 Cactus Spine Road
Phoenix, Arizona

JOB OBJECTIVES

I have been engaged in one particular type of
work now, you see what I'm saying, a good long
time, I mean a lot of people that have been
in this type of work as long as I have aren't
working at all anymore, you get my drift, there.
So I would be very much interested, this point
in my life, in finding myself a new position and
a new title. Even a new name wouldn't be such
a bad thing, you see what I'm saying. Also, a
company in a sort of remote place where I would
be difficult to locate, as being located could
tend to distract me from my job responsibilities.
Also, no sudden loud noises.

EXPERIENCE

1970-1984   International Telegraph, Construction,
            and Amusement Machine, Inc.
            Chicago, Ill.
            Senior Group Head for Administration
            and Leaning
            People with whom the corporation had
            significant fiduciary dealings needed
            a little leaning on from time to time,
            and this was substantially my area of
            responsibility. No big thing, you know.
            You just want people to know, with
            respect to certain trade relationships
            and standing negotiated agreements, not
            to be a fucking wise ass.

1960-1969   Nahant Fraternal Lawn Bowling Society
            and Social Club
            Nahant, Mass.
            Vice President for Drug Deals That Fre-
            quently Erupt Into Violence
            In this position I pursued a particular-
            ly vigorous and aggressive marketing
            approach, taking no shit from anybody.
            On an occasional basis it was necessary
            to see that a few things be taken care
            of, because these were the kind of things,
            if people didn't take care of them, it's
            the people that get taken care of and
            not the things, you take my meaning.

Anthony Avengio - pg. 2

1955-1960   Lucca's Lovely Little Luncheonette
             and Soda Fountain
             Newark, N.J.
             Telephone Order Representative
             You'd be surprised how many take-out
             orders you get, a little place like
             that. We had eight phones going in
             the back at one point. Really kept
             me jumping. I guess the way it is,
             these days, people have to race around
             a lot on the job, they don't want to
             take a long lunch, they might get at
             odds with the boss, you know what I
             mean?

SALARY REQUIREMENTS

Rather than be paid a conventional salary, I
would prefer to lend a mutually agreeable sum
to my employer and be paid back at an interest
rate of 200% per week.

PERSONAL

Age 54. Weight 240 lbs. dripping wet. Excellent
health. Hobbies: Phoenix Men's Not Singing Club.

This is a first-rate resume of the "discursive biodata" variety, in which the applicant is informal and forthcoming about his impressive job history. As an employer, I would be very apprehensive about letting this applicant move on to a competing organization.

CHAPTER FIVE

Job Interviews: An Ugly Business At Best

If you've made careful use of the exercises and resources in the preceding chapters, you now have a round of job interviews lined up—and boy, how I envy you! Job interviews are just about the most desirable experiences available on earth. You can talk all you want about other "peak moments"—trying to return something you bought at a flea market, checking into Sloan-Kettering to get that growth looked at, making a life-size replica of the Alamo out of thawed Lean Cuisine—but, for me, job interviews are *it*.

What actually goes on in a job interview? If you're like most job-hunters, especially inexperienced ones, you've probably been subjected to a great deal of off-putting, intimidating misinformation about the interview process. Relax! In 1983, complaints to the National Labor Relations Board about the use of electrodes on genitals in job interviews decreased *by more than 7 percent*. A job interview, after all, is simply an exchange of information. The interviewer is gathering information about you in order to decide whether to risk his or her reputation and pension by taking a big fat flyer on you or whether to hold on to a secure, comfortable future by getting you the hell out of there. Similarly, you're there to gather information as to whether you'll soon be making a living by scavenging for recyclable aluminum cans that people throw away. So what's the big deal?

It's been said that the "initial contact" period of the job interview—the first five minutes or so—is the most crucial. Whatever takes place for the remainder of the meeting, the first impression you make will set in motion the "interpersonal dynamic" that will determine the success of the interview as a whole. (In the next chapter, we'll discuss how to make the best possible visual impression by wearing the right clothes.) Make these crucial five minutes work for *you* by observing the following principles:

Interviewers like an applicant who's curious about the company he or she hopes to work for. Read memos in the interviewer's "In" box during the interview, and be conspicuous about it. As the conversation proceeds, wander over to the filing cabinet, pop open a couple of drawers and riffle through the folders, mumbling, "Marketing plan . . . projections . . . gotta be in here somewhere . . . ."

Interviewers like an applicant with few starry-eyed illusions about the world of work. Try a straightforward approach: "Let's cut out all the bullshit, okay? We're both just a couple of whores, right? Corporate whores. We put out for whoever pays us enough. Well, fine. You people pay me enough, I'll put out just great. I've been around the block a couple times, all right?"

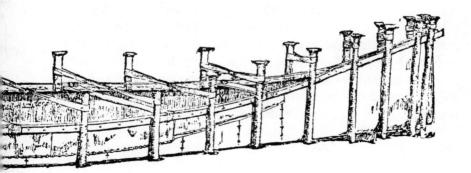

Interviewers like an applicant who will be a good "team player" for the company. Again, the essential thing is to be direct: "Look, I know what's going on around here. I'm not an idiot. I just want you to know, I'm not the kind of guy/gal, you hire me and right away I get antsy and go blabbing to the feds, all right? All I want is my cut."

Interviewers like to feel that an applicant takes the interview process seriously, and has made an effort to arrive on time. It's *not* overdoing things, for instance, to arrive for the interview out of breath, with clothing mussed, a bloodstain on your sleeve, and a telltale bulge under your jacket, gasping, "Goddam receptionist . . . thought she was gonna keep me out there forever . . . reading magazine . . . make me late for interview . . . hadda take her out . . . (block doorway as interviewer rises) . . . I wouldn't go out there right now . . . those .45s make a hell of a mess . . ."

As to the rest of the session, the thing to remember about job interviews is that they *are interviews*. Anyone who's read *Playboy* or *People* magazine, or watched Johnny Carson or Phil Donahue on television, knows what an interview is and how it is conducted. Think of the people you've seen interviewed most frequently: movie and recording stars, best-selling authors, sports celebrities. These people make more money than many emerging nations. So it stands to reason that, by following the example they set in their interviews, you'll come out well in yours. Try the "job hunter" responses in these sample exchanges in front of a mirror:

INTERVIEWER: I see in your resume that you worked for Jerry F. over at Sanitationtronics.

JOB HUNTER: Oh, sure, Jerry—Jerry is a very dear friend, he's a marvelous, marvelous guy and we've had some wild times together—nothing *too* wild [laughs], but . . . you know, he has a terrific—I guess you'd have to call it a facility, for waste dumping . . . it's out past the county line—no, but seriously, the man has a way of getting the best out of you, whether it's a toxic job or a simple slag mop-up, and it's just a thrill to work with him. I love him. I mean it.

INTERVIEWER: Did you really push your last boss out of a moving train?

JOB HUNTER: Yes, and that was some of the *most* fun—I think we have some film of that . . . is that film ready? Can we take a look at that? Oh, good, watch this . . .

INTERVIEWER: Why did you leave your last job?
JOB HUNTER: Mmm. That's an interesting one. [Pause.] I'm very glad you brought that up, because I think that's an area we should be looking at a lot more—I mean, not only why *I* left *my* job, but why people in general leave their jobs, what goes on there . . . there's a lot we're learning, and yet there's still so much we don't know. With a lot of people, I think there's a kind of *restlessness* now, and I think that what's happened to the family has a lot to do with that. Don't you think?

Above all, bear in mind the job you hope to get as a result of the interview. As previous chapters have demonstrated, dumb jobs are easy to get but not worth having, while smart jobs are hard to find and well worth the trouble. Consider the actual responses of two job applicants in recent interviews with the same personnel executive when asked the standard question, "Why do you want this job?"

APPLICANT A: Well, obviously it's a very good job to have. It's a serious responsibility, a good title, a good work environment with what looks like a good-paying job, and of course that's a consideration. But also—I guess the best way to put it is that I feel like this is a job I've sort of been training for, or working up to, at my previous jobs. I feel that I've got the necessary skills together, and I know my way around this kind of work. It's going to be a challenge, but that's what I'm looking for. And I think the enthusiasm of the people here is inspiring as hell, I really do.

Applicant A got the dumb job he was applying for and today is a harried, overworked, intimidated, bullying, impotent alcoholic wage slave.

APPLICANT B: Why I—the job wants to—[twitches]—I warn you, sir—*the Lutherans are bent on conquest!*—The key—*tungsten* is the key, the—*don't breathe on me!*

Applicant B was made the company's Reclusive Eccentric Billionaire in Charge of Bringing in Movie Stars to Have Sex With.

Let this be a lesson to you: when you apply for a job, *make it a smart one*, and tailor your interview style accordingly. If what you want to be is a Macao gun-runner, then begin the interview by back-handing the interviewer across the room, sweeping the office for bugs, and blasting the Selectric II on the desk into the next life with an assault rifle. I don't care if the company you're interviewing at makes religious supplies—dictate the job you're applying for, rather than letting the interviewer dictate it for you. For the rest of the interview, and other smart occupations, see the chart on pages 58-59.

Prohibited Questions

Under recent court decisions, it is illegal for job interviewers to ask certain questions of applicants. These are:

*Is that a full range of managerial and interactive capabilities you have there, or are you just glad to see me?

*Would you rather be smart and miserable or dumb and happy?

*How do you keep a moron in suspense?

*Do you feel that the salary we're discussing will enable you to live reasonably well while you pay for having my basement remodeled?

*Would you skin a human being with a Buck knife in order to increase our market share or brand awareness?

*Are you a cop?

If an interviewer asks you any of these questions, you are automatically entitled to replace that interviewer in his or her job.

The Interviewer says . . .	. . . and you answer—depending on the job you want.				
	$13,500-a-year flunky	**Reclusive eccentric billionaire**	**Macao gun-runner**	**Prize stroker**	**Dewar's Scout**
Do you have some prior experience in this area?	Yes, I've worked in this field for some years now, as you'll see on my resume.	Cholera! Your necktie is *crawling* with it! Rosicrucian scumbag! Get back! Back!	I'm only gonna say this once: Lumumba. Cyprus. Tet Offensive. Now do you want to do business, or do you want to fuck around some more?	(Smile, run hands over coat rack)	Hey, the last time I had any prior experience in *this* area, I was blind for three days! Ha ha ha ha ha ha!
Would you relocate in order to take this job?	I certainly would. I've talked it over with my family, and they agree that it's worth it.	I want all the croupiers wearing live blowfish in their lapels! Big ones! Big live blowfish!	No. Same alley as last time. You people want to start getting cute with me, I can cut a deal with the insurgents, okay?	(Smile, point to chrome sculpture of wobbling skier on desk)	Sure, where am I now? Ha ha ha ha ha ha!
Do you have a lot of management experience?	Yes, as you'll see, several of my references are from people who've worked for me—I think those are just as important as the ones from people I've worked for.	Crepuscular . . . effulgent . . . Dannemora . . .	Yeah, I know a lot of those Japanese management techniques . . . you've seen 'em on the old World War II movies . . . management by water . . . management by bamboo . . .	(Smile, run hands over interviewer's appointment calendar)	Oh yeah . . . managing to find my keys . . . managing to find my car . . . managing to find my way home . . . ha ha ha ha ha ha ha ha!

What were you thinking of in terms of salary?	Well, based on the general range for this kind of job, and on my track record, I think a range of $14,000 to $16,000 would be reasonable.	(point to desk blotter) This has *zinc!* (Eat desk blotter)	Put the paycheck down and walk away from me with your hands behind your head. Nice and slow. Every two weeks.	(Smile, point out features of interviewer's desk)	Salary? Hey, let me get this week's. No, come on, you got last week's. Ha ha ha ha ha ha ha ha ha ha!
You realize, of course, that there are several other applicants for this one opening . . .	I'm sure there must be—it's an excellent job. I think my qualifications give me a good shot at it, but—well, the decision's up to you folks, isn't it?	Judy Canova . . . Black Sox . . . *Holy shit! Hit the dirt!* (Fall to floor)	Make my day.	(Smile, run hands over interviewer)	Hey, I'm not surprised! There are *two of you!* Ha ha ha ha ha ha ha!

"And he spake unto them, saying,
'Let us put on the raiment of
Polly and Esther, with many bright
plaids and checks that are upon
them, and go forth as men of
sales, selling the Lord's word.'"

—Carnegians 2:16

CHAPTER SIX

Dress to Impress

For Men

As important as behavior is, the role of appearance in creating a successful impression at a job interview is just as great, or greater. And let's face it: the average American businessman dresses in a way that is nothing short of disastrous. Why? Because he's allowed himself to be cowed by fashion "experts," designers and sales clerks into accepting a style of clothing that guarantees that he'll fade anonymously into the woodwork just when he most needs to be recognized and remembered. Just look at the colors that so many men choose for their suits—dull "background" colors that are the very essence of forgetability. I call these colors Gutless Gray, Blah Blue, and Boring Beige.

If you want to succeed at the job interview and thereafter, learn the key rule of successful business dressing and learn it well: *The more plaids you pack into your wardrobe, the more power you pack into your image.* A man who's afraid to combine a couple of contrasting plaids in his outfit is probably afraid to meet serious business challenges—and interviewers know it. A bright, colorful

THE "LANGUAGE" OF SHIRT CUFFS

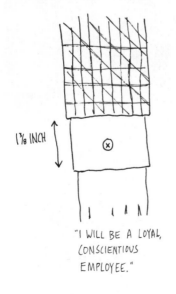

1 3/8 INCH

"I WILL BE A LOYAL, CONSCIENTIOUS EMPLOYEE."

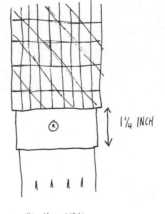

1 1/4 INCH

"I WILL STEAL TRADE SECRETS AND MAKE EXPENSIVE PERSONAL PHONE CALLS."

plaid says *bold . . . Old World money . . . exclusive country club . . . tasty shortbreads,* while a solid gray or blue—or, worse, a Pathetic Pinstripe—says *Oh, excuse me, I must be in the wrong office. Sorry.*

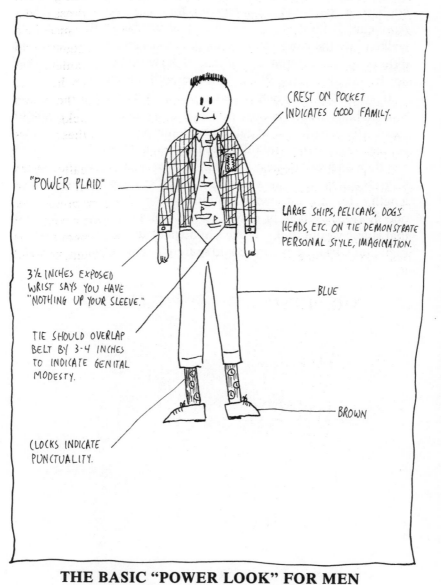

CREST ON POCKET INDICATES GOOD FAMILY.

"POWER PLAID."

LARGE SHIPS, PELICANS, DOG'S HEADS, ETC. ON TIE DEMONSTRATE PERSONAL STYLE, IMAGINATION.

3½ INCHES EXPOSED WRIST SAYS YOU HAVE "NOTHING UP YOUR SLEEVE."

BLUE

TIE SHOULD OVERLAP BELT BY 3-4 INCHES TO INDICATE GENITAL MODESTY.

BROWN

CLOCKS INDICATE PUNCTUALITY.

THE BASIC "POWER LOOK" FOR MEN

There's more to correct business dressing than plaids, of course, as the drawing of the Basic Power Look for Men on page 63 points out. But plaids can make an enormous difference. Consider the case of Applicants A and B (pictured below), who applied at the same company for the same position in sales. Applicant B blew Applicant A out of the water the minute he walked into the room. Was it his past sales record that made the difference? His references? His use of the word "orientated"? Hell no. It was his Power Plaids that turned the trick.

If you study the sample plaids (opposite) you'll soon be able to get a basic business outfit together and move on to fine points, such as the length of shirt cuff that extends past your jacket sleeve. As the diagram on page 62 demonstrates, a difference of even an eighth of an inch can be crucial in this area. Many job-seekers like to grab a Swingline stapler and join the sleeves at just the right length before the interview. Nothing wrong with that, and it's just one more advantage of power plaids—on a "Sappy Solid" suit, that staple would stick out like a blind duck in a duck blind. On the right plaid, trained experts could search for a week without finding it.

APPLICANT A   **APPLICANT B**

KNOW YOUR PLAIDS

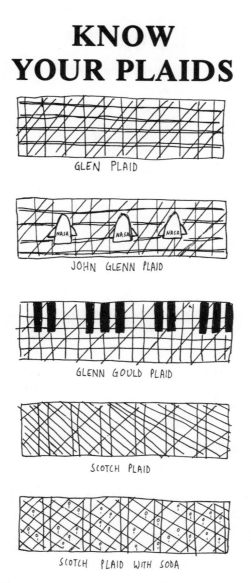

GLEN PLAID

JOHN GLENN PLAID

GLENN GOULD PLAID

SCOTCH PLAID

SCOTCH PLAID WITH SODA

For Women

While men have been doing business as usual—cutting sleazy deals, hitching their pants up with their thumbs, sneaking over to Sears during business hours to eat popcorn and look at power tools—women have been waging a quiet revolution in the American workplace, taking an ever-increasing share of business power and responsibility. They must learn to dress to impress, just as men must.

THE WOMAN'S "POWER SUIT"—
ENDLESSLY ADAPTABLE

THE BASIC LOOK

BLOUSE WITH BOW (WHITE, PALE YELLOW, OR PALE BLUE)

SUIT (GRAY, NAVY, OR BEIGE)

THE "OLD GLOUCESTER"

THE "TIMES SQUARE"

THE "LAST MILE"

And for women, plaids are *not* the answer. This is because women's bodies, on the average, contain 37 percent more curves than men's. (This is not sexism. This is cold, scientific fact.) The result is that plaids worn by women tend to assume the look of "op" art, which has been out of fashion for many years.

As a visit to any modern business office will show you, the successful woman's "uniform" is the Power Suit—blazer and skirt, usually in gray, blue, or beige, worn with a light-colored blouse, preferably with a bow decoration on the front. Studies show that this outfit enables women to command more respect and authority than any other kind of outfit.

However, many women don't work in business offices—and they make the mistake of thinking the Power Suit isn't for them. Thus we see women in factories, or on construction crews, denying themselves the abundant image benefits of this basic outfit. Big mistake! As the drawings on page 66 show, one of the Power Suit's most appealing attributes is its adaptability to non-deskbound occupations.

Then again, many women who do go to the trouble of wearing the Power Suit then turn right around and undo their image by choosing the wrong accessories, before and after the fact. A woman who wants to be taken seriously in the business world, and then wears something as juvenile and un-power-ish as a teenage charm bracelet, has only herself to blame if she doesn't command the respect she's looking for. As the drawings below make clear, the modern working woman's charm bracelet makes more than just a fashion statement: it says S-U-C-C-E-S-S in no uncertain terms.

THE EXECUTIVE
WOMAN'S CHARM BRACELET

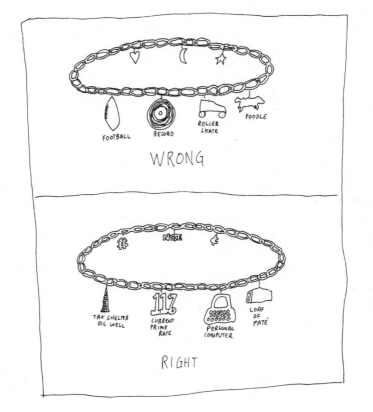

*"Here, look. Just type
in your name. This is
the neat part. Okay...
now push 'Enter.' Okay,
wait... now it's going
to do something really
neat... See? It's saying
'Hello' to you! It knows
you! Is that neat, or
what?"*

> —*A leading computer
> scientist*

CHAPTER SEVEN

Future jobs: Technology and Entrepreneurship

Okay, let's say that this potently helpful, clearly written, life-changing book you hold in your hands has wised you up to the necessity of selecting a smart job over a dumb one. Let's say that you've used the resume-writing and interview-going advice in the previous chapters—advice for which you would have had to pay a consultant *thousands* of dollars—and the job you want still isn't out there. The game shows don't need any new prize strokers for the next two seasons; the splinter group you were running guns to in Macao has gotten hold of a crude thermonuclear device; the Dewar's people have discovered a gold mine—a sloppy-drunk chapter of MENSA in Princeton, New Jersey—and laid off 60 percent of their scouts. Worst of all, the casinos in Las Vegas have all the reclusive eccentric billionaires they need, and you haven't been able to convince any of the small licensed poker clubs in Gardena, California, that they could use a reclusive eccentric worth, say, a few hundred thousand.

So what do you do now? Do you give up, write yourself off as a person, kiss your future goodbye, and take an honest job?

Not so quick. This is a new era we're living in today (Thursday). Americans are doing *their own* niche-making, solution-envisioning, and reality-creating. They've got the gusto. The eye of the tiger. They're going for it. They're dreaming, hustling, networking, shoving their obnoxious gimmicks in decent people's faces. In short, they're becoming *entrepreneurs*—going into business for themselves. (It's interesting to consider the root parts of that word, by the way—*entre* from the French *entre nous*, meaning that the secrets of individual enterprise are known only to a fortunate few; and *preneur* from *preneurotic*, meaning "just about to go crazy from having so much money to spend.")

Many forces have conspired to make this new age of opportunity possible: a technological explosion, the emergence of a "service economy," corrupt district attorneys. It's an age in which a pre-teen computer genius can proudly point to his first million before he can point much else.

How are you going to take your place in this exciting new scene? With an *idea*. Where are you going to find this idea? All around you—in people's shifting, adapting, often stupid, modern life-styles.

Example: any observant person has noticed a significant change in the market for wine over the past few years. Once a beverage enjoyed predominantly by an elite of well-travelled

connoisseurs, wine today is being consumed by a broader market than ever before. There are blind tastings in middle-class suburbia, wine bars in downtown business districts. There are low-calorie wines, wines-in-a-box. And yet, a large segment of the potential market remains untapped. Among blue-collar drinkers, beer is everything and wine is nothing. One theory holds that this is because wine is only for people with refined, selective tastes. This is nonsense. We have seen Orson Welles advertising wine on television, and Orson Welles will eat and drink anything. Another line of argument is that wine "doesn't get you as drunk" as other beverages, but this too is demonstrably false. If wine didn't get one drunk, how would you explain the contents of this chapter? And yet, the market penetration problem remains, and nothing seems to help.

Nothing, that is, until an entrepreneurial mind does some heads-up brain-cranking! Hasn't it occurred to these people that *it's not the wine that's at fault—it's the glass*. That fine crystal wine glass may be great for bringing out taste, color and bouquet, but as a working-class utensil it's disastrously wrong: a snobbish, fragile, intimidating museum piece.

That's why the Keeno-Vino Glass, shown above, is a brilliant entrepreneurial solution to this problem. Put a few dozen million of these babies into production now, and by next year there will be wine in the fast-food outlets, wine in the average guy's lunch thermos, wine in the bleachers at the ball games. And *you* will be looking into checking accounts in the Caymans. Why? Because you had a dream, and went for it.

More ideas, you say? It's *easy* to have ideas when your mind is on the fast track of modern American marketing-think. Consider: *people who are afraid to fly never read in-flight magazines.* A problem? No, an opportunity! Start up *Flite-Fear Monthly* and this large, untouched audience will never have to miss another photo-feature on the surprising new face of Waco, nor another forty pages of crucial Dictaphone advertising. Or how about all the people in this country who have trouble going to sleep, and don't want to take drugs, and don't even send the drugs to me? There's a gold mine here too: a chain of special movie theaters called The Morpheum. The programming? I'd start with Satyajit Ray's *Apu* trilogy, follow it with *L'Avventura*, and build up to an annual Frank Perry Festival featuring *David and Lisa, Diary of a Mad Housewife*, and *Play It As It Lays*. And I'd be *rich*.

Or perhaps the ongoing revolution in financial services such as banking and stock brokerage is your handbasket to opportunity. Hardly a day goes by without news appearing in the business pages of stock brokerage houses offering new money-management checking accounts, or of discount stock-trading desks springing up in savings-and-loans and even department stores. Deregulation has busted this field wide open.

But studies show that there is, again, a large untapped market segment—in this case, "baby boom" young adults who came of age in the socially conscious '60s and early '70s, and who are made vaguely uneasy by their increasingly large incomes—uneasy enough to avoid serious investing as something "square" and "part of the establishment."

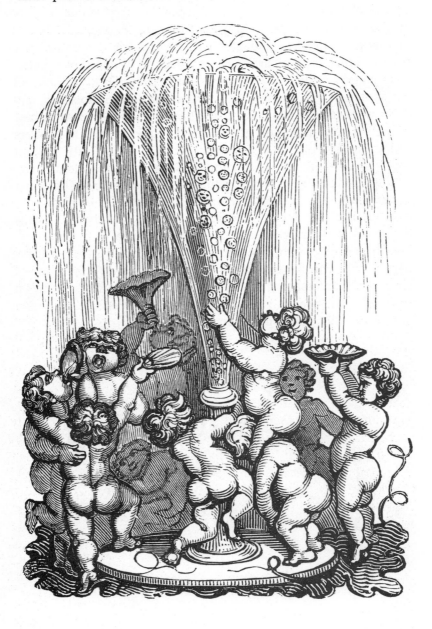

How to reach these people and put their idle dollars to work in the stock market and your own pockets? Easy: *become a Rastafarian stockbroker!* Marketing surveys show that over 60 percent of upscale ex-radicals have been to see *The Harder They Come* at least four times, and fully 38 percent "would feel more comfortable" with an equities salesman who wore dreadlocks, read the Psalms a lot, and smoked as much dope every day as the average American consumes in his or her entire junior high school career. It could be *you*, skanking down to the office every day with a Coptic Bible tucked into your *Wall Street Journal* and racking up walloping sales records. (Being black is useful, but not strictly necessary. The *Big Chill* crowd is very easily persuaded.) It could be *you*, greeting that Cuisinartsy young couple with, "Hail! Hear what I man say! Mek we buy somehundred shares dis new offering Tacky-Tech Industries, seen? Dis yah offering sanctioned, *sah*. I true! Who de SEC bless, nuh man cyaan curse. *Ital* offering! I man no check fi dis Wahner Communications business, that a dread business, that third-quarter Atari loss a go fe be abomination pon de eyes of de Shareholder of Shareholders. But dis Tacky-Tech, way dem earnings projections sight, soon come dis issue a go *spliff two for one!*"

But as terrific as all these ideas may be, and as uncondition-
ally guaranteed to make you richer than hell as they are, they pale
beside the fantastic opportunities presented by the exponential
growth of computer technology in California's Silicon Valley,
Boston's Route 128, and other high-tech headwaters. Don't take
my word for it, take that of a leading career and employment
newsletter: "There is no question that computers, and the related
technology, could be the invisible reweaving of the 1980s!"

"But," you say, "I have no aptitude for mathematics or
science." Big deal! The fact is, *you have to start somewhere*. Just
eighteen months ago, twenty-two-year-old scientist Martin "Lex"

Luther was a mail clerk. Today, thanks to his invention of VisiGoth, the popular software program for plotting corporate takeovers, and CookBooks, the top-rated crooked accounting program, he is fabulously wealthy. And, as you may have read, the inventors of the popular early video game "Pong," before completing their successful prototype, spent months laboring on the development of a game called "Ping," which was intended to simulate "the thrill of minor automobile engine trouble."

So it is with you: you need a "way in." Many starter-outers choose to begin with the classic entry-level job, that of the computer deprogrammer. Just as people-deprogrammers kidnap Moonies, Rajneeshis, and adherents of other cults in order to return them to reality, a computer deprogrammer's typical assignment might be to go to an airport, kidnap a computer that records flight reservations, bring it to a motel, and talk sense to the machine until it stops routing San Francisco-Seattle passengers through Detroit.

But—what with wrestling computers onto moving walkways and enduring the curious stares of Travelodge clerks—deprogramming can be a wearying business. For this reason, you might want to get right to the "hot power center" of the new technology: the expanding, challenging world of computer crime.

Because computer crime is so much higher-tech than other felonies, it's generally considered a "white-collar" crime, of the sort more likely to result in a book contract than a jail term if you're ever caught, which you probably won't be. Celebrated computer criminals have netted as much as $10 million at a time, just by programming computers to "call up" other computers on telephone lines and move money around, or by "sneaking" into bank computers and transferring funds into their own accounts. And, since computers have powerful memory storage systems at their disposal, the criminal is in a position to steal 1967 dollars, which are vastly more valuable than the present model.

"But isn't this kind of thing for scientific doubledomes? I can't balance my checkbook on a coke scale," you lament. Well, even without fancy knowledge or equipment, you could get in on this bonanza. In fact, just as doctors and lawyers make their time expensive by mastering impenetrable jargon, big-time computer criminals are loath to admit that, once the scientific mumbo-jumbo is stripped away, many of their crimes can be committed perfectly well by laypeople, *without using computers*.

For example, before there were computers, long skeins of office mathematics were handled by adding machines—which, being noisier than computers, actually have something to *say* when they get on the phone. One ingenious noncomputer criminal, Carter W., arranged the following call between his second-hand Burroughs adding machine and its counterpart in the back offices of a large strip-mining and carcinogen conglomerate:

CARTER W.'S MACHINE: Chick chuk chir*ring* chukka wuk *ching*!

CONGLOMERATE'S MACHINE: Puck pock rucka ducka ching a ling chir*rup*?

CARTER W.'S MACHINE: Clik clakkety wukka chuk *chingle* ding!

These sounds, of course, are too technologically complex to make sense to the untrained ear. But suffice it to say that, even as Carter W. hung up the phone, half of the conglomerate's annual profits were on their way to the savings and loan branch where he maintained his NOW account. Today, Carter W. lives in a splendid villa in the Santa Cruz Mountains, has shrewdly invested the proceeds of his caper, and is welcomed into social circles that once sneered at his lack of a complete last name.

Another example? Sure. Ordinary computer criminals are content to "sneak" into a bank's computer from a remote location. But if you time your move to occur during the so-called "sweet spot" hours between 10 a.m. and 3 p.m., you can go "inside" the bank itself, with no sneaking at all. Within seconds of entering, you'll find yourself "in line"—a noncomputer term meaning that you'll be spending a good deal of time behind a woman depositing $58 in pennies, a man trying to untangle two months' worth of overdrafts, and an elderly lady who needs twelve money orders and speaks only Croatian.

When you arrive at the teller's window, do *not* hand him or her a crudely lettered holdup note of the sort that was fashionable during the pre-cybernetic age. Instead, hand over a modern-day holdup *printout*—a stack of blue and white paper, accordion-folded, thick as a phone book, and crammed with dense computer language. As the teller and his or her co-workers huddle over this confounding mass of heat-printed alphabet soup, searching for some familiar, reassuring mention of a gun or an admonition to cooperate and not get hurt, you'll be free to collect all the money you like from the drawers and vaults. (Don't neglect to avail yourself of any cookbooks, road atlases, or calendars the bank may have on hand. Insiders regard these as "valuable free gifts.")

Being a successful entrepreneur is the apex of contemporary American business aspiration. When you have achieved this status you will be eligible to:
- Work your own hours.
- Listen to motivational cassettes in your car.
- Wear garish I.D. bracelets with "DAMN I'M GOOD" engraved on them and diamond lapel pins that say "#1."
- Call men "babe" and women "guy."
- Lease a private Learjet (named for the early entrepreneurial personality King Lear).
- Have a hair transplant.
- Buy a briefcase with a phone scrambler in it.
- Have a bodyguard who once worked for Joey Bishop.
- Have a valet who worked for Tony Martin and can tell you what Tony sings in the shower.
- Go to a fat farm.
- Hint darkly about your "silent partner" in the Mob.
- Go public.
- Collect Leroy Neiman.
- Dance embarrassingly in velour jumpsuits.
- Drink Fresca and vodka.
- File fraudulent tax returns.
- Proposition hotel maids.
- Give inspirational talks to civic organizations and high school assemblies.
- Flee the country.

*"There is only one route
to success, and that is the
route of persistent effort,
honest representation, and
sincere good will. Ha ha
ha ha ha ha ha ha ha ha ha
ha ha! Whoo! Ha ha ha ha!"*

—Robert Vesco

CHAPTER EIGHT

Career Change: A "Predictable Passage" of Mid-Life

John DeL. was a successful automobile executive. Not content to function within the established corporate structure, he struck out on his own, with an independent company building cars in Northern Ireland.

And yet, he felt that "something was missing." It wasn't financial security he lacked: John DeL. had built up a healthy IRA retirement plan (as well as a substantial IRA work force, who had almost learned how to wire a car's electrical system without using plastique). But he wanted new challenges, new excitement. "During my business career," he says, "I had experienced intense stimulation. Now I wanted to pass some of that stimulation on to other people. I felt that I could help to make that stimulation available in many places—the mail rooms of large record companies, for example, and at certain singles bars where the bartender was cool. I began looking for people who could help me to bring this about. Surprisingly, some of these people turned out to be connected with the government. I've always been more or less of a maverick, you know, so I didn't really welcome the involvement of those people—although it appears now, with one of the possible arrangements we're looking at, that the government may end up covering my overhead for several years down the line. I have to say, I was very, very surprised."

Mary C. held an executive position at the Bendix Corporation, which manufactures William Bendix, star of the old *Life of Riley* television series. But, she recalls, "I knew there had to be something more. For one thing, I felt I needed more access to the really top people. I wanted to be present at critical meetings on things like mergers. And also, I felt that it would increase my effectiveness enormously if there were thirty or forty reporters and photographers jumping at me like a pack of crazed hyenas every time I so much as went out for a cheeseburger. Otherwise, you don't really feel you're having an impact." By forming a strong association with a decision-making executive on a higher management tier, Mary C. soon was able to "get down to business" issuing denials, declining comment, and giving unctuous interviews only to journalists to whom she could have sold the Brooklyn Bridge before dessert. "That way," says Mary C., "when I became ready to make my career change, the board and stockholders seemed to know it even before I did."

Lech W. was an electrician at a busy shipyard. He enjoyed his work, but "I needed to *expand*. I felt I wasn't really using my 'people skills' in that job. For example, I always felt that the Pope and I would have a lot to talk about if we got together. When you think about it, being a shipyard electrician is a lot like being a Pope. I mean, he might be out on a balcony a lot, and I might be up on a loading crane, that kind of thing.

"But it didn't seem like that was going to happen just through my knowledge of wiring. I mean, the Pope needs something rewired, they've probably got a whole squad of guys over at the Vatican, can do that." But by "networking" with several million other workers who were also interested in career changes, such as having fewer skin searches in their careers, Lech W. was able to "liaise" with personalities ranging from the Pope to brutal secret police goons with huge truncheons.

"Something was missing" . . . "There had to be something more" . . . "I needed to expand" . . . These are the increasingly familiar refrains of the mid-life career changer. Often, as people make their passage from their "Threshold Thirties" into their "Dead Reckoning Decade," they experience a "change of life," in which their job needs and desires change, and a new career becomes an irresistible need. Some of the most commonly asked questions about this change, and the answers, are:

When will this change happen to me?

It varies. No two people have the same mid-life experience, but these guidelines generally hold true. If you are a teacher, the need for a new career will strike immediately after you finally get tenure. If you are a civil service worker, eighteen months before you would have been eligible for a pension. If you are an employee of a worker-owned company, six weeks before a buyout would have made you a millionaire.

Will I experience "hot flashes" during this change of life?

Yes. An example would be: "Hey, here's a hot flash for you:

nobody wants to hire you, because they're afraid you might fall over and die soon."

Will a new career bring me the fulfillment I've been looking for?

Sure it will. Sure.

The most pressing question, of course, is what one's second career should be. Some people, unfortunately, choose to go to extremes in this matter. A brawny steelworker will walk out of the mill one day, never to look back, and attempt to become a high-priced caterer of society affairs, telling his clients, "Yeah, what I'd do, to start off, I'd get a lot of salmon mousse in here, I mean like a fucking *ton* of salmon mousse, like enough salmon mousse to sink an aircraft carrier, you know what I'm saying?"

Such abrupt and radical transitions are almost always ill-advised. The trick in career-changing is to make the change part of a *complete life plan*, a conscious design that addresses itself to your ultimate life goals. If your ultimate life goal is to stop wrongdoers, for example, you may want to choose a second career as a wrongdoer and then retire immediately.

An outstanding example of a successful mid-life career change is that of Dr. Herbert McInerney Featuring Fluffo, of Metuchen, New Jersey. "For years, I had a very pleasant life working as a ventriloquist," says Dr. McInerney Featuring Fluffo, a cheerful, energetic man in his early fifties. "Kids' parties, banquets, an occasional TV shot . . . but I started reading some of that Norman Cousins stuff, you know, about how laughter can help people recover from illnesses, and I always felt that I might have a little knack for internal medicine, so I thought, what the hey, why not combine the two, and I became a surgeon. And I'll tell you, it's the best decision I ever made—it's not so much a second career, it's more like a second *phase*, because I'm able to use the old along with the new. I'll have a patient on the table, where I have to remove the pancreas, let's say, and I'll have the incision open, and I'll say, 'Let's see how this pancreas looks.' And then I have this Peter Pancreas voice that I've worked up that's really quite good, and of course it seems to be coming from right inside the patient, and I'll have it say something like, 'Gosh, let me out of here, Doctor! You wouldn't believe what this guy *eats*!' Some of those people just about jump right off the table," Dr. McInerney Featuring Fluffo chuckles. "You can't tell *me* that a patient under anaesthesia doesn't know what's going on."

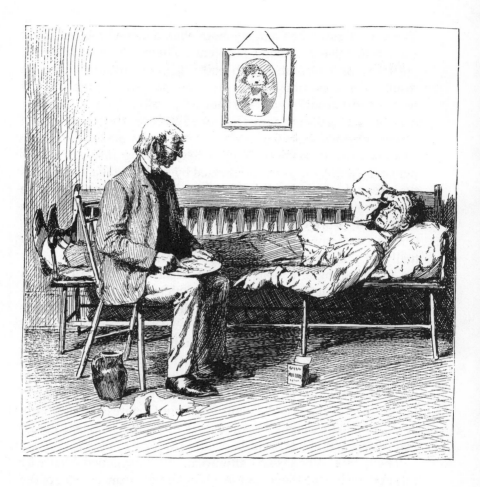

CHAPTER NINE

Job Burnout, and How to Get It

There are times when a new job, or even a career change, is not enough to solve a person's problems. There are times when the pressures of a high-stress job and a high-achievement lifestyle result in a condition called *job burnout*, which one leading psychologist describes as "the shortest possible distance between a life of making decisions at a Fortune 500 corporation and a life of making Popsicle-stick trivets down at the happy place." Driven to success by our ambition-mad society, "hung up" on a self-punishing perfectionism, and dizzied by such social upheavals as the "sexual revolution," the "information explosion," and the "fall carnival of values," the burnout victim soon becomes an exhausted, work-obsessed shadow of his or her former self. (Private detectives and CIA agents suffering from burnout actually *do* shadow their former selves, hoping to catch them in the act of alienating affections or being affectionate toward aliens.)

If job burnout is caught in time, the victim can be restored to a well-rounded lifestyle. But if burnout is ignored, or treatment postponed, the result is often a disastrous break with reality. Take the case of Mr. G., a popular women's hairdresser at the Dimensions in the Tops of Rich Women's Heads beauty salon in Encino, California. Working long hours for several years to perfect his techniques and build a clientele, Mr. G. had "made it": his version of the pageboy cut—"a little Congressional, a little corruptible"—was only one of several "hit" hairstyles he created, and his appointments were booked up weeks in advance.

Then, one Wednesday afternoon, "it" happened—halfway through rinsing the Placenta Placebo shampoo from the hair of the wife of an important Universal Studios executive, Mr. G. wheeled around, struck a dramatically foppish pose, and announced to the entire salon, in a Hispanic patois that had never before been heard from his lips, "Thanking you! Thanking you so much! We are for your entertainment the special Apache dancers Lope and Lupe de Vargas—Miami to Cuba! Thank you! Thanking you so much!" Then he grabbed the hair of his startled customer, pulled her from the chair and flung her toward the far wall, leaving a three-and-a-half-foot Ultrasuede skid mark on the Congoleum.

A trained observer could have seen Mr. G.'s troubles coming a mile away: too many years of looking for the "perfect combout," of listening to the problems of women named Rhoda and even Estelle, had precipitated a classic case of job burnout.

Are you a candidate for burnout—or, even worse, are you already suffering from it without realizing it? Take some "quiet time" to ask yourself these ten questions, giving yourself three points for each "yes" answer:

1. Do you work in a high-stress job? (see chart below)

2. Do you easily become annoyed when people contradict, interrupt, or divorce you?

High-Stress Jobs

Manufacturing
Transportation
Sales
Office Work
Design
Communications
The Arts
Utilities
Sports
Wholesaling
Retailing
Service (food, lodging, etc.)
Entertainment
Finance
Farming

Low-Stress Jobs

Official greeter
Society matron
Ed McMahon
Refrigerator magnet

---

3. Do you feel a "lack of intimacy" with your alderman?

4. Do editorials in *The New Republic* seem "dry, dull, uninteresting"?

5. Is your spouse "fooling around" with "somebody new," having "unimaginably wild sex" behind your back because you're too preoccupied with work?

6. Are you sure?

7. Are you "too busy" to take up scrimshaw?

8. Do you take a belaying pin into meetings with you?

9. Does filling out your income tax returns seem joyless, like something to be "gotten through" rather than something to take pleasure in?

10. When shaken, do you make a dry, tinkly noise? (This is a chief indicator of burnout in household lightbulbs and, interestingly, works with people as well.)

If your score was 12 or higher, you are in serious danger of burning out. At this stage, unfortunately, the remedy is rarely something as simple as a vacation or a change of job responsibilities—your entire physical and emotional "infrastructure" is in fragile shape. What's needed, most likely, is an extended stay at an intensive care facility specializing in the job burnout problem. Perhaps the best-known such facility is the Nu-You Burnout Clinic and Last-Chance Pecan Roll Stand operated by Dr. Armacost Annaleg in Vague Throbbing Sensation, Kentucky. At the clinic's sprawling, "distinctively strip-mined" grounds, a brochure states, a victim of job burnout can "achieve distance from the work-related 'mind-set,' reassess personal priorities, get 'back in touch' with feelings of identity and self-worth, and purchase a variety of fine nut confections and detailed road maps of the tri-county area."

Arriving at the clinic's "administration module"—a handsome, aluminum-sided structure with a "WIDE LOAD" banner attached to one end—a visitor is greeted by Dr. Annaleg himself, a LaSalle-trained psychologist who, at thirty-five, remains spry, mentally acute, and deeply fascinated by fast money. "Most of my patients are people who made it here just in time. A lot of them are about two creative-meeting follow-up memos this side of bongo-bongo land, you can see it the minute they show up here," he says, leading his guest past the Nu-You's day room, where two haggard-looking middle-aged men sit at a card table, shelling nuts of some kind.

"Pecans," Dr. Annaleg explains. "It's a kind of tactile-motor-therapy thing. Those two were up against each other in a big takeover battle a couple of months ago. Antitrust actions, full-page ads full of backbiting innuendo in the *Wall Street Journal*—a real mess. They both snapped right at the height of the thing, and their boards sent them both here. I got them in here, I said, 'You guys are real cute or something, right? A couple of wise guys. Real sharp operators. One of my assistants turns his back on you, you'll prob'ly stick a homemade Cross pen in his back, get him to sign over his proxies, right? People think I'm crazy, put you two guys in the same room—they figure if you don't wipe each other out you'll get the others all stirred up, and try to pull a buyout on me one night. Well, forget it. There's only one CEO here, and that's me. You try any funny stuff, I'll have the Justice Department subpoena certain of your former fiduciary officers so fast you'll be begging me to get back in here.' Look at 'em now—shelling nuts, laughing . . . these guys come out here, they get a whole new outlook.

"It's still an experimental field, burnout therapy," Annaleg continues, leading the visitor from the administration module to the clinic's outdoor hydrotherapy sump. "At first, I was totally barking up the wrong tree. For a few years there, I had the theory that burnout was just an 'aggravated phase' of cookout—you know, barbecuing. So I would lead these encounter groups where I would talk about 'letting go of your hibachi,' or I would make the patients walk around wearing these signs that said things like 'Starter Fluid Junkie'—charcoal sobriquets, essentially.

"But gradually I came to realize that the word 'burnout' is very misleading in that regard, and what we're really dealing with here is the end result of 'Workaholism,' of over-involvement in the job.

Some people believe in letting the patient withdraw gradually, but I make them go 'cold worky.'

"That lady over there—" he points out a goosebumped woman treading the cold, muddy water of the sump—"she was a media buyer at an ad agency in New York. Had a big account, one of the major lines of kids' breakfast cereals. Little chocolate-marshmallow-alphabet-leprechaun things, you know. And she was working eighteen-hour days, seven days a week, and one day, *wham*, she put their whole fall print schedule into *Teen Honeys in Bondage* magazine. Classic burnout case. She's coming along . . . but it's pathetic, some of these people, when they first come in here—you get guys on their knees, *'Please*, doc, you *can't* cut me all the way off . . . lemme have a few file folders, a Telex, *any*thing . . . .' They're sick, and they don't realize how sick they are.

"Every fresh batch that comes in, it's the same story—some time during the first week, I catch them sneaking off together, and they don't think I know what they're up to. I know what they're up to, all right—they're having a department heads' meeting. Or I'll tell one of them about our movie night or something and he'll say, 'That sounds really feasible, let me get on the horn and bounce that off a few people. I think we could get some excitement going there,' and then you have to cuff him around a little. It's a cry for help, really.

"What we've come to realize here is that you have to get these people away from abstract things—you have to put them back in touch with simple, basic activities. Shelling nuts is an excellent example—it's like they're solving a little problem, getting to the inside of things. Or rolling little caramel logs around in the nuts, so the nuts stick to them. That gives them a sense of coherence, of things holding together, which very often has been missing from their lives. Sweeping up in our little store out front gives them the sense of sweeping all that pain and confusion out of their lives. It's true that they pay a lot for this therapy, but it's also very effective. After six weeks here, a vice-president of a television network can be working an orangeade machine on his own—probably the most useful thing he's ever done. These people are producing so many pecan products by now that we've started a wholesale operation, a mail-order thing with an 800 number in *The New Yorker*, the whole works."

Not surprisingly, Dr. Annaleg has had no patients from the "smart job" categories outlined earlier in this book. "Nope, no prize strokers to speak of—no gun-runners either. Mostly, it's your big-deal executives. And it's so unfortunate, you know, you look at these people from time to time and you think, if only they had snuck off to a few more Bruce Lee triple features at the height of their busy seasons, they wouldn't be here today."

After they're discharged from the clinic, Dr. Annaleg is asked, do patients succeed at applying what they've learned here and moderating their work habits accordingly?

"Discharged? What in the hell would I want to do that for?" the psychologist parries. "Here, you want a praline?"